I0456700

ISBN: 978-0-578-00537-9

This book is a gift from:

_____

To

_____

Illustrations by Laura Sweeney.

Discover Courtly Love through Shakespeare

Laura Sweeney, Ed.D.

William Shakespeare (1564-1616) epitomized the magic of courtly love in his romances, ***Romeo and Juliet*** and ***A Midsummer Night's Dream,*** along with his incorporation of traces of courtly love in his tragedies, for he must have celebrated the authors Dante Alighieri (1265-1321) and Francesco Petrarch (1304-1374) who preceded him in Italian literature rather than in English literature. In fact, Shakespeare took refuge in romantic Italian and Greek settings for his theater rather than always placing his characters in English settings, chiefly when he wished to depict courtly love. Not only does Shakespeare's drama reveal men to be courtly lovers, but it also empowers women as courtly lovers with the help of ancient gods and goddesses in the Athenian landscape of *A Midsummer Night's Dream,* a romantic comedy about love. Through the empowerment of women, he parallels Dante and Petrarch to show there is more to love than marriage preordained by Renaissance fathers' force. Shakespeare then plunges into the equally stunning earthly realm of fairies which is a mirrored alter-image of Beatrice's and Laura's Heaven.

Italian Baldassare Castiglione (1478-1529), facilitated the tradition of courtly love during the Renaissance with his book entitled *The Courtier* in which he demonstrated how unattainable love could lead man on the path to God and ultimately to love of all humankind. Although many readers attribute the birth of courtly love to Castiglione, Dante preceded him with Dante's *Vita Nuova*, the story of how Dante existed purely to experience the convivial smile of his beloved Beatrice whom he had first met as a child and who later married and died at an early age. Notwithstanding her ethereal state, Dante continued to take refuge in most devout love for the rest of his life—to improve himself through the contemplation of his beloved Beatrice. Here are some words from Dante's Inferno in which he describes angelic Beatrice:

"Then she was silent, and I began: 'O lady of virtue, in whom, alone, humanity exceeds all that is contained in the lunar heaven, which has the smallest sphere, your command is so pleasing to me, that, obeying, were it done already, it were done too slow: you have no need to explain your   wishes further. But tell me why you do not hesitate to descend here, to this centre below, from the wide space you burn to return to.'"

(Kline, Dante, 10)

Much like Dante loved Beatrice, Francesco Petrarch loved Laura from the time he met her when she was six-years-old and he constantly contemplated her image as he aimed to receive her blessing, even after her marriage to another man and premature death at age thirty-eight. Petrarch declared Laura was divine even when she was no longer with him on earth:

Soleasi Nel Mio Cor

"She ruled in beauty o'er this heart of mine,
A noble lady in a humble home,
And now her time for heavenly bliss has come,
'Tis I am mortal proved, and she divine.
The soul that all its blessings must resign,
And love whose light no more on earth finds room,
Might rend the rocks with pity for their doom,
Yet none their sorrows can in words enshrine;
They weep within my heart; and ears are deaf
Save mine alone, and I am crushed with care,
And naught remains to me save mournful breath.
Assuredly but dust and shade we are,
Assuredly desire is blind and brief,
Assuredly its hope but ends in death."
(Higgenson translation, Petrarch)

These sonnets summoning ethereal women paved the way for both Castiglione's mode of chivalrous loving and Shakespeare's courtly romance. Hence, Dante and Petrarch were true originators of the courtly tradition which in due course empowered Shakespearean women as well as men to show their true feelings exclusive of prearranged marriages of the times. Petrarch's soul reached honorable altitudes due to his recognition of his beloved Laura and her acceptance of his love, much like Romeo sought to attain honor in loving Juliet. Another Shakespearean character named Helena sought honor from recognition by her beloved Demetrius in *A Midsummer Night's Dream*. These one-sided relationships were the seeds and fruits of courtly love that inspired great writers and artists from the 1300s through the 1600s and even in secret today.

Courtly love, known as the Italian *"amore cortese"*, was a noble yet prohibited, affair characterized by ritualistic adulation, gift giving, adultery and secrecy. In this context, the lover focused completely upon his lady's majesty while he kept his affection secret from others. That the woman might have been married to someone else did not deter her suitors since sacred love was considered to have been the extraordinary, single force that could elevate man to his highest spirituality. The lover contemplated ways in which he could gratify his sweetheart and receive her approval which was manifested solely through her loving gaze. Love was the most important event in life as it transported lovers to a state of total elation. Thus, honorable conduct was guaranteed (Thompson 1).

Courtly love was an acceptable form of adoration in Shakespearean times when it was customary to love from afar for the mere pleasure of being in love. Today, such love from afar would be regarded as silly or childish. The magic of courtly love manifested itself from the distance when the lover found his beloved beyond his reach due to her higher economic status, her unavailability, her marriage arranged by parents, or other obstacles. Young ladies similar to Juliet knew it was best to obey their fathers' orders to marry husbands chosen in the context of prearranged marriage. Choosing for oneself, as Juliet chose Romeo and as Desdemona (in *Othello)* chose Othello, demonstrated lack of respect for their fathers. Disobeying the rules of prearranged marriage resulted in tragedies; whereas, maintaining unconsummated courtly love would not have resulted in penalties. Consequently, Cassio's platonic love for Desdemona in the tragedy, *Othello,* would have been perfectly acceptable then because it was nonphysical. However, today's society derides platonic love even when courtly love does still exist. The difference is that the modern-day courtly lover remains quiet about such chivalrous feelings of religious and sacred love.

When Romeo and Juliet speak of love, they speak of souls meeting. These two lovers go beyond spiritual contemplation of courtly love when they marry in the church. Their real focus, aside from consummation of the relationship, is spiritual fortification and drawing closer from the mutual blessing of the beloved's acceptance. Rosaline, Romeo's first love, was too lofty for him and, in the eyes of the Elizabethan audience, may have been an unattainable love object. Rosaline instantly loses her appeal when Romeo encounters tangible Juliet and determines Juliet is the real love within spiritual reach. Romeo's courtly love ensues at first sight. It is the one and only love to outshine all and to carry on both in life and after death.

Today, such emotional extremes appear foolish. Rather, people express sentiment more akin to Juliet's nursemaid's version of love, which is dutiful, sexual, and physical rather than spiritual. Juliet's nursemaid advises audiences that women function as men's helpmates in accomplishing practical tasks grounded in obedience. However, a number of men today share Mercutio's attitude that there is little connection between sexuality and love, that men should be predatory and hide all sentiment. Mercutio takes sex lightly while teasing his peers and Romeo about their sentiments.

Friar Laurence represents another viewpoint of love, that of the Father, the Son and the holy Church. He determines that only God sanctions love and mends all ills. He believes marriage between two oppositional families (the Capulets and the Montagues) will heal members of the community if sanctioned by God. Shakespeare deliberately manipulates each character to represent a viewpoint pertaining love and sexuality. Each character presents options to Romeo and Juliet so that the youths can make an informed choice for themselves.

The representation of courtly love in Shakespeare's dramas is not limited to romantic stories. There are also traces of courtly love in tragedies such as *Othello*. For instance, the protagonist, Othello believed that Cassio's courtly love of Desdemona consisted of physical intimacy. Yet, Cassio's love never took sexual expression and remained a means of platonic, spiritual support for both Desdemona and Othello. Cassio loved and served Othello as much as he cared for Desdemona. Conversely, Othello gave in to wicked, earthly Iago, incarnate of the Devil who tempted his jealous nature—his tragic flaw—resulting finally in everyone's downfall. Naturally, in return for Cassio's kindness, the Venetians granted courtly Cassio rulership over Othello's domain while Othello and Desdemona passed away tragically. Othello's refusal to acknowledge religious and platonic love resulted in everyone's downfall from grace in front of the Venetian court. (Note that Cassio and Desdemona began the drama as Venetians in the home of courtly lovers. Othello was an outsider Moor who got tricked out of embracing his true courtly ideals by the evil Iago who questioned the validity of love.)

Friar Laurence does not readily accept the existence of courtly love and questions how a young man's love swiftly changes from loving one woman to another overnight when he believes love, like God's love, should be constant. The good Friar examines the validity of courtly love as opposed to traditional marriage preordained by one's own family. He believes it impossible to experience love at first sight unless love unites two families with the assistance of God. The church supported his medieval viewpoint, still existent today in some areas of the world, that fathers must choose daughters' spouses and that daughters should never question their fathers' choices. Friar Laurence believed love to be unchangeable; however, Romeo challenged the Church's tradition with his instantaneous romance, describing Juliet as if she were Petrarch's Laura:

"One fairer than my love? The all-seeing sun
Ne'er saw her match since first the world begun."
(Shakespeare, *Romeo and Juliet*, 1.2)

Juliet reinforced the existence of sacred love declaring she must immediately marry Romeo and consummate the marriage as soon as possible so the church could not annul her nuptials. Consummation of marriage occurred not for sexual motivation but for legitimization of nuptials. Juliet was merely thirteen-years-old and would have been considered too young for marriage unless it had been prearranged for financial and social motivations such as family alliances. She, too, praised her beloved Romeo and became a young, female courtly lover when she spoke of how Romeo was much like elements of nature including the stars:

"Give me my Romeo; and, when he shall die,
Take him and cut him out in little stars,
And he will make the face of heaven so fine
That all the world will be in love with night,

And pay no worship to the garish sun."
(Shakespeare, Romeo and Juliet, 3. 2)

Romeo is even brighter than the sun. These words come unexpectedly from a young woman's lips. Here Shakespeare empowers women as protagonists who treat men as beings endowed with qualities belonging to angelic, heavenly redeemers—customarily women. Shakespeare characterizes women as they have never been represented before. This shocking and empowering drama grows to be a precursor to Romanticism which later follows the Renaissance age and confirms women as active researchers of love. Juliet says that once Romeo becomes one with nature, all the world will love the night. She is creating irony in stating he is also like the sun. Night and day juxtaposed as opposites possibly signify two parts are at once whole.

The nurse, with her simpleton point of view, tells Juliet she should pretend she is not married to Romeo and just marry Paris as her parents would have her do, follow her father's rules as do all good daughters, even when there is not love. The nurse believes girls must do that which is convenient because love is physical and monetary as opposed to spiritual. She ignores the detail that Juliet has already married Romeo and that a new marriage would be polygamous. The nursemaid only sees convenience. Her lower social class causes the nurse to make these ignoble suggestions that surprise modern audiences. She literally tells Juliet to deceive all in the name of convenience. Besides, Juliet must decide between loving Romeo who is now a criminal who killed her cousin and loving a wealthy noble named Paris who is not a bad gentleman.

Signor Capulet reveals himself a cruel and uncaring father who would abusively give his young daughter away to someone she does not love. Capulet envisions love as a duty to be fulfilled by the woman. In other words, men rule over their wives and daughters must be controlled at all times, even controlled when the daughters go to church or make confessions to priests. Capulet asks too much when he expects a young girl of merely thirteen years to marry a man she does not know because this man has wealth. One cannot help but question whether Signor Capulet would have forced his daughter to marry Paris if he had known she would have been guilty of polygamy. That is doubtful, so one asks an additional question: Why did the youths continue to lie to their parents? As a parent, one cannot help but think the youths should have been honest with their parents and that they should have lived happily ever after if Romeo and Juliet merely told the truth. Moreover, Signor Capulet told Tybalt (the play's antagonist) that Romeo had a good reputation and that he did not wish Tybalt to harm Romeo. He did not seem to hold the least grudge against Romeo and wanted to please the Prince to protect family's reputation in the community. Instead, Tybalt, who was the equivalent of a modern day gang member, held a grudge against all Montagues based on failure to examine facts. Tybalt symbolizes mindless adherence to group-think. He held responsibility for the deadly fights to ensue, resulting in the deaths of Mercutio, and later, Romeo and Juliet.

Fortunately, this is merely fiction, not to be confused with the real world. Stage actors are simply representative of personality profiles, and it is not easy to explain the fictive youths' lies, but sacred, courtly love seemed to be even stronger than the bonds that tied people to parents and to the material world. Pre-Renaissance writers and artists alike took pleasure in the creation of these idyllic, heavenly ladies like Juliet, Laura, or Beatrice—ladies who embodied angelic and healing qualities for their audiences. Such romanticized women, whether real or imagined, inspired many great works of art in various mediums. It seemed yearning for an idealized feminine presence also exemplified passionate and deviant lust, characteristics obviously contrary to sacred love. For instance, adoration consumed Romeo to the extent he sacrificed himself for love, hoping to join his lady in the Heavens with an audience that put faith in an afterlife that was better than life on earth. In due course, the sacred and more earthly paradigms wrestled for Shakespeare's dramatic attention. The fictive lovers manifested their love equally in earthly stage settings as in heavenly stage settings. These were the realms of both fairies and angels.

Shakespeare fully comprehended the most famous, Italian sweethearts, Beatrice and Laura, both of whom died during Dante's (1265-1321) and Petrarch's (1304-1374) lives, but who continued to inspire these literary geniuses throughout their lives. Dante's and Petrarch's beloved women were adored and honored in poetry long after their deaths. Even today, their spirits seem to impose their timeless beauty upon modern readers. Indeed, the courtly lover prized only one woman and did not shift allegiance simply because she was no longer alive. As a result, the courtly poet transformed his lady into a symbol of the Christian Mary's magnitude, a leader of the Cult of the Virgin.

Romeo, figment of Shakespeare's imagination, ultimately transcended the test of time in the hearts and minds of readers from the Renaissance onward. Romeo symbolizes all elements of sacred, courtly love as his physical body and that of his lover are compared with nature itself. Romeo sees both the sun and moon, two contrary forces like the Yin and Yang, in Juliet and he, too, is a mirror image of her:

"But soft! What light through yonder window breaks?
It is the East, and Juliet is the sun!
Arise, fair sun, and kill the envious moon,
Who is already sick and pale with grief
That thou her maid are far more fair than she."
        (Shakespeare's *Romeo and Juliet*, Act II, 2-6)

The following description of Juliet exemplifies the way a courtly lover would speak of his beloved. Romeo utters these words upon first sight of his young lady:

"O, she doth teach the torches to burn bright!
It seems she hangs upon the cheek of night 45
As a rich jewel in an Ethiope's ear—

Beauty too rich for use, for earth too dear!

So shows a snowy lady trooping with crows,

As yonder lady o'er her fellows shows.

The measure done, I'll watch her place of stand, 50

And touching hers, make blessed my rude hand.

Did my heart ever love till now? Forswear it, sight!

For I ne'er saw true beauty till this night."

(Shakespeare's *Romeo and Juliet*, I.V. 45-60)

Juliet mirrors Romeo with her description of Romeo who is compared with the night:

> Come, gentle night, — come, loving black brow'd night,
> Give me my Romeo; and when he shall die,
> Take him and cut him out in little stars,
> And he will make the face of Heaven so fine
> That all the world will be in love with night,
> And pay no worship to the garish sun.
> (Juliet, Act III, scene 2)

Italian Baldassare Castiglione, contributed to the invention of the tradition of courtly love during the Renaissance with his book entitled *The Courtier* in which he described how unattainable love leads to praise of God and in turn to love of all humankind. In other words, the mere process of loving lifts the lover to heavenly heights. Loving one another is a course of developmental action that one improves upon through contemplation of beauty. Such thoughts serve to elevate the spirit and increase awareness of the needs of humanity.

Romeo and Juliet's love helped them attain oneness with the entire physical world as they endlessly compared one another with natural elements like the sun, the stars, and the moon. Throughout the play, they envisioned each other within the landscape and were carried to blissful heights as they became one with the environment. Nevertheless, love does not always turn out blissful in Shakespeare and these two star-crossed lovers ended their lives tragically.

In spite of everything, the story of Othello points to the tragedies of jealous love. Othello and Desdemona initiate a spiritual, loving relationship with true marital devotion regardless of Desdemona's father's disapproval. Othello adores her, while Desdemona in turn proves to be equally devoted to him, but Cassio, one of Othello's devotees, turns to Desdemona for help, revealing strong, platonic love for both Desdemona and Othello. Cassio has no intentions of consummating his friendly relationship and is most dependable, intent upon pleasing Othello. Nonetheless, devilish Iago interposes himself between Othello and his honorable Desdemona because Iago is jealous of Othello. Othello succumbs to Iago's lies since Othello's weakness is jealousy and possessiveness of his beloved wife. Shakespeare shows audiences how adoration shifts to hate over night when a liar like Iago interjects himself between the couple. Perhaps Desdemona believed too much in love, not knowing that Iago would have lied about her relationship with honest and honorable Cassio. Innocence finally leads to her downfall since she has no idea courtly love could give birth to marital hate:

"If it were now to die,
'Twere now to be most happy, for I fear
My soul hath her content so absolute
That not another comfort like to this
Succeeds in unknown fate."
(Shakespeare, Othello, lines 205-209)

In Hamlet, audiences observed a dastardly twist on courtly love whereby Hamlet's uncle loved Hamlet's mother. Courtly love turned sour when they crossed the lines to explore family love that was off limits. The two appeared outwardly to show genuine affection but the malevolent uncle would have done anything to physically possess his beloved Queen, including the murder of her husband (his brother), unbeknownst to her. Had it not been for the ghost of Hamlet's father who appeared to Hamlet one evening, no one would have discovered the truth about the King's death and about the extremes that the uncle went to in order to kill his beloved queen's husband. In the courtly tradition, killing the spouse would not have been a consideration, and Hamlet's uncle was consequently punished by reaching a tragic ending, accidently killing his new wife with the poison he had intended for his nephew. Then both he and Hamlet died in representation of how evil might bring the downfall of an entire family. Bad deeds returned threefold to malevolent lovers for the reason that real courtly lovers would have sought only to become better people so as to write poetry and love the whole of humankind.

In other words, there were certain boundaries that people did not cross without repercussions in the literary world of fiction.

On a much lighter note, *A Midsummer Night's Dream* represents the transition of a timid, young woman named Hermia, who is property of her father, about to be forced to marry Demetrius whom she does not love, into an independent woman who gets the man of her choice. Little-by-little, Hermia becomes a free woman because she follows her heart by taking off into the fairy's forest to be with Lysander, the one she really loves. At the same time, another courtly-lover named Helena seeks her own beloved Demetrius who is supposed to marry Hermia. Helena tells Demetrius that Hermia is running off from home to meet Lysander since Helena hopes to follow Demetrius into the woodlands. She believes she will benefit from the mere sight of Demetrius and servitude to him. Somehow, seeing him and following him will elevate her. Helena embodies female courtly love because she wishes merely to gaze upon her beloved and that in itself suffices—no need to consummate this relationship. In such manner, *A Midsummer Night's Dream* evokes the powers women have to court men and to oppose their fathers' wills when fathers wish to give their daughters' hands away in prearranged, loveless marriages.

In Athens, Hermia refused to marry Demetrius whom her father had chosen because she already loved Lysander, but she had only four days to obey her father's wishes, or else she would have died. Hermia and her constant beloved Lysander had audaciously gone against the grain of the times, including legal authorities, something unheard of and an ingenious move on Shakespeare's part! Meanwhile, her friend, Helena, had also loved Demetrius at length, as was known by all, and even begged him to abuse her by treating her like a dog! She knew very well that Demetrius did not care for her. Fortunately, the God Oberon felt sorry for Helena and helped her attain the love she sought through magic. No longer did Demetrius ignore her, as often happens when women chase men. Rather, he followed after her, and for awhile, even Lysander—under the influence of magic—chased Hermia too!

Initially, Hermia asked many questions of Helena, such as how Helena had been able to invoke powers of courtly love upon Demetrius. Hermia described Helena in a manner that again is much like Dante or Petrarch would have praised their ladies:

> "Call you me fair? that fair again unsay.
> Demetrius loves your fair: O happy fair!
> Your eyes are lode-stars; and your tongue's sweet air
> More tuneable than lark to shepherd's ear,
> When wheat is green, when hawthorn buds appear.
> Sickness is catching: O, were favour so,
> Yours would I catch, fair Hermia, ere I go;
> My ear should catch your voice, my eye your eye,
> My tongue should catch your tongue's sweet melody.
> Were the world mine, Demetrius being bated,
> The rest I'd give to be to you translated.
> O, teach me how you look, and with what art
> You sway the motion of Demetrius' heart."
>
> (Shakespeare, *A Midsummer Night's Dream*)

Hermia's discourse depicts the viewpoint of the courtly beloved quite well since she compares eyes to stars and she compares the voice of another person to great melodies. Beloved Hermia seemed to attract Demetrius and take his heart away from Helena. Possibly, Shakespeare wished to show how dreamers are often guided by mere figments of their dreams, such as fairy-imagery, and how sentiments quickly change based upon outside factors. Shakespeare shows the audience how imagination becomes confounded with reality in the woodlands where the fairies reside.

The star-crossed lovers unknowingly cross paths with the king and queen of the fairies

in the woodland, Oberon and Titania, who had quarreled over the possession of a little Indian boy and whether the boy would follow the male god or female goddess. The two gender-based powers struggled for dominance, but Titania stood her ground against Oberon. In order to force her to give in, Oberon called upon Puck to invoke the magic of the Love-in-idleness flower which would make anyone fall in love with the first person he or she saw upon waking. This, Oberon thought, would be hilarious revenge against Titania, but Oberon, feeling sorry for Helena, eventually told Puck to make Demetrius fall in love with her via use of the flower. Thus, what began as two mortal women chasing men, turned into men chasing Helena for the sheer delight of seeing her. Meanwhile, Titania fell under the spell of the Love-in-idleness flower when Puck sprinkled it upon her and she was smitten with a donkey-like, clown-like actor who set out alone into the woodland, possibly an alter-image of Shakespeare. The actor remains central to the story because he is the one whose imagination and dreams are too intense to be understood by the rest of contemporary Elizabethan society.

Upon awakening from her spell, Titania realized the foolishness of enchantment and that love is often blind when directed at people who are like donkeys. Titania momentarily became a courtly lover when she loved the donkey-actor, bestowing many gifts upon this man who looked like a beast. After all, her love was blind like love can be in real life! Both she and the actor-donkey may represent confusion between what is reality and what is not real, the mundane world versus the solo creator. One ponders why the mythological creatures would philander with the creative actor in the first place!

While under Oberon's spell, both Demetrius and Lysander acted like chivalrous lovers as they did everything in their power to woo Helena. Meanwhile, Helena believed they made fun of her since she was unaccustomed to male attention. Even Hermia did not understand the sudden change in the men's hearts which possibly represented how outside factors such as dreams impact the heart and mind. Perhaps this is an allegory in which Shakespeare suggests that love is also a magic spell in which the enchanted lover does not see the real beloved. Courtly love does appear superficial, especially when lovers find those they love do not return love; however, courtly love calls upon men and women alike who are both poets and dreamers. This empowerment of women as lovers distinguishes William Shakespeare's work from so many other writers of his day.

For example, Helena, although female, symbolized a new breed of woman, aiming to entice Demetrius with her own initiative. She could not take *no* for an answer, and she was content just to follow her man although he chased after his betrothed Hermia. Unlike many of Shakespeare's stories, *A Midsummer Night's Dream* ends happily because Shakespeare bestowed the power of courtly love upon women and freed women from prearranged marriages in English literature. Moreover, true lovers triumph!

Juliet shared affections similar to those of Helena in that they were powerful female protagonists who did not betray their own heartfelt desires. They fixated upon their loves and performed all necessary actions to succeed in getting their men. Juliet received the assistance of the nursemaid who represented mindless and simple women's duties. She also received assistance from Friar Laurence who represented spirituality of the traditional church; whereas, Helena (a Greek rather than Italian) obtained assistance from the God Oberon, his helper Puck, and the fairies of the forest in a pagan fashion that was analogous to Christianity.

Juliet was like a saint to bless her lover's hand and make him overflow with extraordinarily pure, spiritual love. Once married and in love with Juliet, Romeo could no longer quarrel with Juliet's cousin Tybalt because Romeo had experienced salvation through love. In fighting with Tybalt, Romeo acted spontaneously out of loyalty to deceased Mercutio, his friend. He temporarily forgot his allegiance with Juliet in his angry fit of passion, and this was Romeo's tragic flaw leading to his own downfall. Only later did Romeo realize that he should not have made the rash decision to fight to avenge Mercutio's death. Having acted irresponsibly, he had put his own marriage and new wife at risk.

Not until he consummated his relationship with Juliet did he leave town, and this meant Juliet took on the role as the emergent romantic protagonist because physicality in itself implies existence of a much later romanticism. Nevertheless, upon Romeo's return from banishment, Romeo saw Juliet in the tomb which was like a "womb" of death—more irony—because Juliet's form became light amidst darkness. Again, she seemed to be Laura or Beatrice. It seemed she beckoned Romeo to the other world, and all he could think of was to join her in a new heavenly realm which seems absurd to readers today.

The Elizabethan audience did not view the lovers' impending deaths in the same manner as audiences would have viewed deaths today, so Juliet and Romeo, in some respects, looked forward to joining one another in death where they thought they could console one another forever in Heaven. Although the protagonists would have preferred life together, death was the second best alternative to living without each other.

The average age of death during the 1500s was extremely young, so the audience might not have felt death was as tragic as modern audiences view it now. The Capulets and the Montagues faced punishment in that their children died and (fictive) Romeo and Juliet would not produce the next theatrical generation. Hatred ended their bloodline, but the audience, along with the Capulets and Montagues, realized how absurd it had been to pass their hatred down to younger generations.

Such tragedy as *Romeo and Juliet* moves audiences by example so participants will learn from destructive actions played out upon the stage. Knowledge and insight come from suffering along with the characters and putting oneself in their shoes. Audiences leave the play with a sense of enlightenment and willingness to consider the results of their own actions. Theater serves them as a form of therapy and coaches audiences to live ethical lives, even more so than if they had seen a movie production of the same play. Drama becomes public ritual in which a wide array of emotions is acted out without doing harm to others leaving an open forum for discussion. It is a passage from fear to healing, from mystery to understanding.

Life in the times of Shakespeare was just a passage to the next step and a passage asking what life means. Romeo and Juliet, Helena and Lysander, all passed from a world in which the father controlled his daughter to the new realm of courtly love and then on to the realm of Romanticism in an ongoing evolution of English literature. Audiences learned that the family unit was inadequate in commanding controls upon children's attitudes in love and marriage, that the will of the sacred, courtly lover in the depth of passion would triumph over the forces of society, including the forced marriages and the domineering family unit.

Petrarch's Laura remains the real precursor of Romeo, Juliet and all courtly lovers. Petrarch permeated the sonnets he wrote with courtly love and passion that carried the reader to great heights inspiring writers such as William Shakespeare. Indeed, Petrarch's description of Laura was written prior to Shakespeare's description of Juliet:

> "She was unlike the earthly, mortal things,
> As one who cared for heaven, nothing else.
> My soul that burned and froze under her spells,
> Wishing to go with her, opened its wings."
> (Petrarch)

Does this not sound like Romeo and Juliet speaking of one another? Laura's ability to enchant Petrarch is the key to romantic art and poetry.

Shakespeare contrasted the earthly world of the nightingale with the spiritual world in which Juliet saw herself "dead inside a tomb" much like Laura. The world in which humans lived was nurtured by the earth while elevated religion and religious love carried humans into Juliet's realm of love healing the soul. Romeo and Juliet was a tragedy of contrasts between the earthly and the spiritual, the body and the mind; whereas, Midsummer Night's Dream was grounded in earth packed with fairies and pagan gods.

A Midsummer Night's Dream remains much more uplifting than *Romeo and Juliet* with the integration of country fairies and gods who interfere with humans' emotions. It seems the God Oberon and his assistant, Puck (the eternal bachelor archetype), prefer to show the absurdity of humans in blind love when they do not recognize the imperfections of the beloved. What games do these sprites play to transform Renaissance lovers through courtly romance? These sprites remind audiences that there does exist magic, both above and below, in which courtly lovers triumph from within their own imaginations.

Audiences must take the positive values embedded in these dramas and live their lives as fervent enthusiasts for courtly love. Shakespearean protagonists are eternal so take heed before weeping! Alas, literary lovers are everlasting!

Love-Personality Profiles

Do these characters remind you of people you have met or feelings that you have had?

Romeo – Romeo is an idealistic, courtly lover who puts love before all things in life. He does not stop and think about other things going on in the world.

Juliet – Juliet is an independent, young lady who is very quick to make decisions. She questions why she has to marry the man her father has chosen for her. She believes that love and making a choice for oneself is what counts, but she does not stop to consider that her father might listen to her if she tells him the truth about Romeo.

Nursemaid – She is Juliet's caretaker, a practical worker who accepts women's traditional roles as caretakers.

Benvolio – Benvolio is a young man who always tries to be good and do what is right. He represents sensibility, good will, and ethics. Benvolio enjoys pleasing others and is good at presenting the facts as they happened.

Signor Capulet – Signor Capulet is an overbearing father who learns a lesson about listening to children. He also learns to regret his ongoing feud with the Montagues.

Mother Capulet – Juliet's mother obeys her husband and lets him make all the decisions, even when he is wrong.

Signor Montague – Signor Montague is sensible man, but adheres to the family feud. He does permit his son, Romeo, to have some freedom because he is a young man.

Tybalt – Tybalt is an irrational antagonist and trouble-maker who does not think before acting. He adheres to group-think mentality.

Mercutio – Mercutio believes love need not be romantic. He is also a joker and makes fun of women. He is a loyal friend and a barrel of fun.

Othello – Othello is romantic but quick to jealousy and possessiveness. He believes anything Iago tells him and does not consult his wife about suspected and untrue infidelities. (Othello)

Iago – Iago embodies pure evil and meanness in the world. He tempts others to do bad things through trickery. (Othello)

Cassio – Cassio is a courtly lover and friend in the pure platonic sense. He is truly devoted to his master and lady. He maintains a positive outlook and is ultimately rewarded. He is blind at times when he does not see bad in others.

Desdemona – Desdemona is a romantic woman who leaves her homeland and father before considering the dangers of romantic love. Her father claims she will be unfaithful to her husband because she was first unfaithful to her father. Desdemona is true to her husband and virtuous throughout the drama, but she pays a price for her husband's jealousies. (Othello)

Helena – Helena is a young woman with the characteristics of a male, courtly lover. She does not consider herself attractive and pursues her man openly. (A Midsummer Night's Dream)

Hermia – Hermia refuses to marry Demetrius who has been chosen by her father. She is headstrong although she risks her own life to be with Lysander. (A Midsummer Night's Dream)

Oberon and Titania – These male and female gods pose a conflict against each other but make peace so that all can live harmoniously. (A Midsummer Night's Dream)

Puck – Puck is the eternal bachelor with a sense of humor. He assists Oberon by sprinkling dust upon lovers to impact their decision making. (A Midsummer Night's Dream)

Works Cited

Best, Michael. Shakespeare's Life and Times. Internet

   Shakespeare   Editions, University of Victoria: Victoria, BC,

2001-2005   <http://ise.uvic.ca/Library/SLT/intro/introcite. html>.

Visited   [December 20, 2008].

Bryson, Bill. Shakespeare: The World as Stage. New York: Harper

   Collins Publishers. 2007.

De Grazia, Margreta and Stanley Wells. The Cambridge Companion

   to Shakespeare. Camdridge: Cambridge University Press.

   2007.

Greenblatt, Stephen. Will in the World. W.W. Norton & Company,

   Inc.: New York. 2004.

Kline, A.S. Dante — The Divine Comedy. England.   23

December   2008 <http://www.tonykline.co.uk>

Muse, Mark. Petrarch. <u>Selections from the Canzoniere and Other Works</u>. Oxford University Press. 1985.

Sadlon, Peter. <u>Francesco Petrarch and Laura De Noves.</u> 21 December 2008 <<u>http://petrarch.petersadlon.com/contact.html</u>>.

Shakespeare, William. <u>The Riverside Shakespeare</u>. 2nd ed. Boston: Houghton Mifflin Company, 1997.

Thompson, Diane. 2006. <u>Courtly Love Study Guide.</u> 24 June 2006 <<u>http://novaonline.nvcc.edu/eli/eng251/amourstudy.htm#history</u>>

Tretsidder, Megan. <u>The Secret Language of Love.</u> San Francisco: Chronicle Books. 1997.

Viegnes, Michel. 2006. <u>Space as in Love in the Vita Nuova.</u> 22 June 2006 <<u>http://www.brown.edu/Departments/Italian_Studies/LD/numbers/04/viegnes.html</u>>.

Laura Sweeney, Ed.D.

Creativity Coaching Available at www.creativeartcoaching.com